Kel   ellogg, Steven

uch Bigger Than Martin

Much Bigger Than Martin

MUCH BIGGER THAN MARTIN

Story and Pictures by
STEVEN KELLOGG

Dial Books for Young Readers / New York

Published by
Dial Books for Young Readers
A Division of NAL Penguin Inc.
2 Park Avenue, New York, New York 10016
Copyright © 1976 by Steven Kellogg
All rights reserved
Printed in Hong Kong by South China Printing Co.
COBE
8 10 9 7

Library of Congress Cataloging in Publication Data
Kellogg, Steven.
Much bigger than Martin.
[1. Brothers and sisters—Fiction.] I. Title.
PZ7.K292Mu   [E]   75-27599
ISBN 0-8037-5809-X   ISBN 0-8037-5810-3

For Kim

Sometimes it's fun being Martin's little brother.

But I hate it when he says, "Let's form a line. The biggest is first. The smallest is last."

Then he makes me play his stupid games.

When we go to the beach with his friends, he says, "You're too small to swim to the raft."

And when he cuts the cake for our dessert, he says, "The biggest person gets the biggest piece."

Once when his friends were there, I was playing basketball.
Martin said, "Better luck next year, shorty." All those
big kids laughed.

I wished that I could grow bigger than Martin.

Much bigger!

I tried to stretch myself.

Then I tried watering myself.

Then I remembered that Grandpa said, "Apples make you grow!"

I told Martin my plan. He said I'd grow into a giant apple.

He said he'd put me in a circus and become famous.

"You'll be sorry, Martin," I said.

"When I'm a giant, I'll grind your bones to make my bread."

I ate every apple, but I didn't grow at all.

I just felt sick.

When Martin screamed, *"Dinnertime!"* I said, "Get out or you'll get bitten by a sick giant."

Mom heard me groaning. She said, "Why did you eat all those apples?"
"So I could grow bigger than Martin," I told her. "*Much* bigger!
As big as a *giant!*"

Dad said, "Why do you want to be bigger than Martin?"

"So I can go to the raft with all the kids," I said.

"And divide the cake so that I can get the biggest part and Martin gets one crumb.

And make a basket so easily that Martin and his friends will never laugh."

Mom said, "If you were a giant, you'd be too big to fit in the house."

"Besides," said Dad, "when Martin was your age, he was just your size. You're wearing his old blue pajamas!"

When Martin came to bed, he said, "Sorry you feel like a rotten apple."

Then he said, "Tomorrow I'll give you a surprise and tell you a secret."

The surprise was a new basket that Martin and Dad put up just for me.

Then Martin told me his secret. He said, "When I was your age, I couldn't reach that high basket either."

So Martin and I were friends again.

But the next day he said, "Let's play ape hunt. I'll be the hunter because I'm bigger, and you can be the little ape who gets captured."

I said, "That doesn't sound like much fun. Besides, I'm making something in the garage."